The Shy Groundhog

Once there was a round brown groundhog.

He lived in a round brown hole in the ground surrounded by tall green grass.

When Fox would come around,
then...
Down down down into the ground
Mr. Groundhog would go.

Where he liked to
sip his tea,
smell the air,
cuddle his blanket,
and look at the clock.

This was the way
he thought it should be.

But when Fox wasn't looking...

Up up up he would go.

Out first would pop whiskers
followed by nose,
finally belly,
then wiggly toes.

He'd giggle and dance, frolick and prance.

Happy, he was, and feeling quite free,
because there were no prying eyes to see.

No, nothing that would disturb his play
and that's the way he would like it to stay.

Groundhog liked to carry on this way,
why not wiggle every day?

One day at first, next two and then three.
Soon would be four days,
there should have been more days...

What something perchance would interrupt this dance?
An unexpected visitor with his unwelcome glance...

It was Fox!

And peeking over the grass,
what did Fox see?

It was that fluffy dancing Groundhog!
The sight filled him with glee.

Do you know what Fox
was about to do?

First Fox grinned, then he giggled.
His whiskers wobbled and jiggled.

His laughter erupted in the end,
for this lavish jollity
he could not comprehend.

Groundhog heard Fox laughing
abruptly stopped dancing.
No more,
no more,
no more prancing!

The laughing
from Fox
had made him sad.
It was time to end the fun he had had.

And so it was decided,
with cheeks blushing red
He, quickly, quietly, lowered his head.

Down the hole he scurried,
off off to bed.

Now safe in his home, all tucked in cozy blankets.

Free to dream
of times he had had, when he was happy.

This made him quite glad.

Ohh! But next morning there came a surprise,
when a most colorful singing butterfly
came fluttering by!

Groundhog knew at once that she was quite neat.
The song she sang was fantastic.

The melody lifted him right past his feet.

Groundhog followed the melody,
up up and out
where he could now see Butterfly
flitting about.

Groundhog admired that she was so free
and so he invited her over for tea.

After tea they would
giggle, wiggle,
and sing in the sun.

One day at first,
next two,
and then three.

Soon would be four but...
something was wrong.

That old Fox had come sniffing, hearing their song.

Quick!
Groundhog gasped.

You must stop flapping and quiet the singing.
No more giggles or wiggles.
No more dancing.
Forget the frolick and prune the prancing.

If Fox sees us he might laugh.
We must do everything to avoid this gaffe.

That was okay, or so Butterfly thought.

Because Groundhog was scared
and although she was not,
down, down they went and prepared their tea, hot.

It was no problem
for Groundhog to hide.

He even felt happy with Butterfly
by his side.

The days went by without a tune.
One day at first, next two, and then three.
Soon would be four
but something was awry...

Butterfly felt funny and wanted to cry.

Outside the sunshine was shining on flowers.

But Butterfly could feel inside
a rain cloud rising for hours.

She ached for the breeze,
loops in the sky,
the buzz of friendly bees.

But Groundhog was shy.

Groundhog saw Butterfly
was losing her color.

He wondered,
why should she be sad?

Look at all the nice things that we had.

There is
a clock on the wall,
a chair in the hall,
a blanket in its spot,
and our favorite copper pot.

Groundhog said cheer up Butterfly,
let us have another tea.

Everything is the way
it should be.

Butterfly decided
she would not cry.

Instead
she let out one long sigh.

Then told Groundhog
all the things
that bothered her so.

They quickly made a plan and
up, up
they go.

Out first popped their whiskers,
followed by noses
finally bellies
and don't forget toeses.

There was dancing
with giggles,
plenty of wiggles,
for sure some
flipping and flapping
maybe even
a little clapping.

Groundhog had fun
with all the play.

Although he felt quite nervous,
was this okay?

You see he was thinking,
what if Fox did see?

All the laughing he'd be doing,
all at me...

But Groundhog saw
Butterfly's color was back.

He must no longer fright,
even if old Fox
would see this sight.

It was then that he decided
the way things would be
would not be the way
he thought they should be.

Sometimes a butterfly just needs to be free.

They went on this way for
one day, two days, three days, four days.

And many more days.

You see,
Groundhog had realized
that every so often
funny Fox might get his peeks.

But...

A butterfly without freedom
is worse than red cheeks.

28408712R00033